ECHO IN THE
DISTANCE

By:
Shayla Michelle

Published by Melanin Origins

PO Box 122123; Arlington, TX 76012

Copyright 2023

First Edition

Library of Congress Control Number: 2022911795

ISBN: 978-1-0880-3931-1 hardback

ISBN: 978-1-0880-4138-3 paperback

This book is dedicated to my parents Linda and Mike Reaves Jr., my husband Shawn, teachers Jean Norville and Robert Gundlach and the always supportive Mona Lisa Lanier and Bro. Lee Freeman.

Thank you for believing in me, supporting my dreams, and encouraging me to write.

He bellows boldly.

The sweet sound of anticipation rolls from tongue to lips to dance in a distant echo.

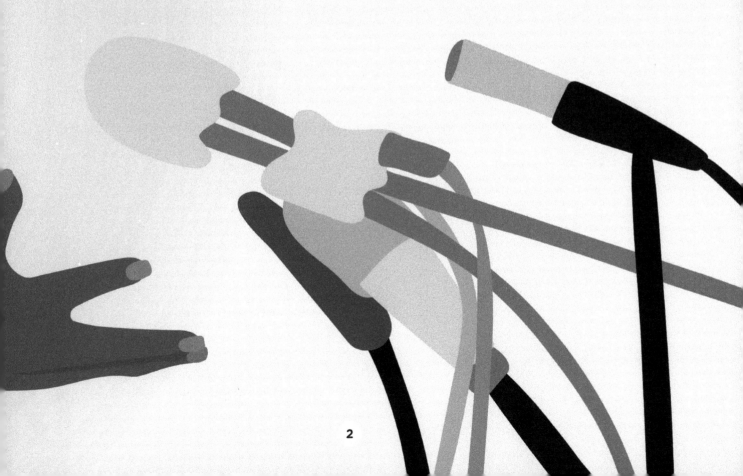

His body trembles as his words flow freely into air.

Voice tearing into tangled blue skies
parting the thick clouds of ignorance
with words resonating towards the sun.

5

Do you hear the echo in the distance?

6

It runs within the crowded River of Watchers,
gushing through the horizon.
Waves of endless observers edging it onward…

9

Just look as they roar!
Watch their hands ring wild with applause!
Watch their eyes gleam glad with the promise...
that tomorrow's sun should yield a brighter day!

Just watch!
His eyes, so stern of fearless design
unwavering in the surge of promise that arises.

He looks ahead.
The creep crawl of tremulous times
is mounting in the wind.

12

Just listen as the thunder grumbles
each rumble of resistance cackling
in the clouds!

Watch the clouds as they fill with rains
of frustration tip-tottering...

13

as the
Drip drop
Drip
of tears
drops
down the faces from the eyes...

the Watchers' eyes....

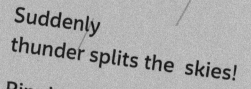

Suddenly
thunder splits the skies!

Ripping hearts, persecuting lives, slitting the evil, dismembering the lies, devouring ignorance in passionate cries, engulfing injustice entangled in time, swallowing fear in fragile minds, digesting change, desegregating the times...

17

18

People are people,
not color-coated crimes!

21

When all has been spoken,

the staggering winds have blown

and battered men and women still stand...

Just listen...
Listen...

23

Do you hear the
echo in the distance?

24

It's knocking on the horizon...

The timeless tap of
progress pounds
from past
to present
to now...

25

26

Now,
I am a face in a River of Watchers,
captivated, captured in the sweet sound of anticipation
lapping against my ear...

A tugging whisper...
pulling at my mind!
Anticipation tears
at my soul,
untangling the clouds
within me.

29

The Voice is now within me...
mesmerizing my mind.
Words that run with character,
words enveloped by a rush of
color are made manifest in the peeking sun!

I am that sun after the storm.

My rays,
the sentiments once hidden in time;
Truth
Acceptance
Understanding,
the outstretched arms that reached...

teaching the lesson that rolled
from tongue to
lips to
transcend time.

People are people,
not color-coated crimes...

36

People are people....
just listen...

listen...
Do you hear the echo in the distance?

40

It's the dream.

ABOUT THE AUTHOR

SHAYLA MICHELLE is an Emmy award-winning tv news journalist with more than 15 years in broadcasting. She graduated from Northwestern University's Medill School of Journalism and was named the top broadcast student in her graduating class.

During her freshman year, she entered and won the university's Written Expression Competition in honor of Dr. Martin Luther King Jr. She first performed "Do You Hear The Echo In the Distance?" during the university's Martin Luther King Jr. program at Pick-Staiger Concert Hall. The audience included keynote speaker Dr. Cornel West. So impressed by the piece, West asked if he could use the line "People are people not color-coated crimes" in future speeches.

Invitations to perform at churches, events and universities followed. Now decades later, Shayla is excited to connect and inspire readers around the world. To learn more about Shayla, book her for an event, follow her journey, or leave a review, visit

www.EchoInTheDistance.com

Printed in the USA
CPSIA information can be obtained
at www.ICGtesting.com
LVHW060427130424
777320LV00002B/2